SNOWED IN LOVE

CONNOR WHITELEY

No part of this book may be reproduced in any form or by any electronic or mechanical means. Including information storage, and retrieval systems, without written permission from the author except for the use of brief quotations in a book review.

This book is NOT legal, professional, medical, financial or any type of official advice.

Any questions about the book, rights licensing, or to contact the author, please email connorwhiteley@connorwhiteley.net

Copyright © 2024 CONNOR WHITELEY

All rights reserved.

DEDICATION

Thank you to all my readers without you I couldn't do what I love.

CHAPTER 1
16th December 2023
The French Alps, France

Even after seven wonderful days of looking out over the stunning mountain range in front of him, Carter Robinson still couldn't get over how damn beautiful it all was. He was sitting on one of the mountain hotel's great brown little sofas that was only large enough for two people, but Carter was currently alone.

He really liked how smooth, soft and expensive the brown fabric felt against his fingers as he sat on his hands to keep them warm in the late afternoon air that was certainly a lot colder than earlier.

It was amazing how the icy temperatures could return so quickly when the sun over the Alps had surprisingly enough brought a little warmth only a few hours earlier.

Carter just rested his snow-booted feet on the expensive glass coffee table in front of him as he marvelled at the sheer beauty of the mountain landscape. All together the mountains looked like sharp twisted daggers rising up from the icy cold ground with a thick blanket of snow covering each of them.

He supposed to some people that might have made them seem scary or menacing, but he only found them interesting, exciting and he had really enjoyed exploring them over the past week. His mum, dad and his big sister Katie had gone to a local French town today to finish up their tourist shopping, and Carter might have been gay but he was so not the shopping type. Not that his lovely parents believed that for a single moment.

Carter had to admit he might have skied a little too hard yesterday trying to beat Katie down the various slopes, so he was feeling the pain in his legs today. But he had still flat out loved the day. Him and Katie had laughed, laughed and had done even more laughing all through yesterday so much so that he had wondered when his face was going to break even with the protection of the skiing googles.

The icy cold wind howled gently past the hotel behind him that was nothing more than a massive dome of glass with the reception, kitchen and main entertainment areas. Then everyone had their own little cabin away from the main buildings.

Carter had really enjoyed sharing with his family. Not only because of the extra body warmth and heat in the cabin but also because it was great fun. They had spoken, laughed and played so many board games that Carter was surprised how much he had missed his family over the course of his degree where he hadn't seen too much of them.

"Can I get Sir anything?" a young woman asked in a posh-looking thick coat with the hotel logo on.

"No thank you," Carter said. "But thank you anyway,"

"Of course Sir. Just summon me if you need anything,"

Carter nodded his thanks and smiled. He had already known this before he had come to the hotel, but it was so clear this place was English-owned and not French in nature. Because if the French ran it then it would have felt a bit less snobby, fake and it wouldn't have felt as clinical as it did.

It was why Carter was sitting out here instead of indoors with the rest of the guests. He was the only one out here and he certainly didn't mind that at all.

The entire outdoor area was empty, cold and too silent with only the howling of the wind for company for a normal person to want to come out here. And Carter really didn't mind that because soon his family would be back and he get to hear all their great stories about the town.

And Carter didn't doubt for a moment that his family would have some stories to tell. They would have probably gotten lost, gotten stuck or something bad would have happened.

Carter might have been on the top of the Alps in

the freezing cold, but he just knew that he was safer here than with his family. His family were magnets for trouble and that was one of the many things he flat out loved about them.

Carter noticed the long lines of Christmas lights wrapped around the metal railings of the decking area and that was another reason why he was glad to be outside. The beautiful little cabins and the reception area and the entire main hotel building were just covered in great-looking decorations.

He loved Christmas, he seriously did but he did want just a little break in the Alps from all the endless Christmas music that played on endlessly in the background. It was great but he understood the importance of moderation after this week.

As the sweet aroma of hot chocolate, lightly spiced ginger and rich sticky caramel sauce filled his senses, Carter looked over at a young straight couple that had decided to brave the cold. And Carter forced himself not to roll his eyes because they looked deeply in love.

Carter couldn't deny the young woman looked okay in her thick black coat, long black leggings and a Russian-style hat. But she was nothing compared to the hot sexy hunk of a man sitting next to her and started kissing her as soon as she had placed her sickly sweet coffee on the table.

Carter wanted to look away but he couldn't. He couldn't take his eyes off the hot hunk she was kissing and as Carter's wayward parts flared to life, he really

really wished there was another hot gay guy here so he could have some very gay fun on his final night at the resort.

But what were the chances of that?

Little did Carter know that him, his family and the entire resort were just about to find out exactly how likely that was.

CHAPTER 2
16th December 2023
The French Alps, France

As Jenson Bench gripped the side of the 4x4 Land Rover in the back seat as their driver from the airport drove them up the immense Alps towards their hotel, Jenson was really starting to wonder what the hell he had set himself up for.

This was meant to be a wonderful family getaway and a celebration and Christmas present because Jenson had now graduated from Kent University with a Masters in Clinical Psychology, mental health as he explained it to everyone, last month. But he was really, really starting to regret agreeing to this trip with his parents and two brothers and he looked down at the sheer drop below.

The Land Rover moved slowly up the mountain and Jenson forced himself to take a deep, relaxing breath in the icy cold, damp, refreshing air. That was proving a lot harder than he wanted to admit.

He supposed despite the roaring of the engine, the protesting of the wheels and the crumbling of the rock around as they inched forward, that the entire Alps were rather impressive.

All around them the huge beautiful mountains covered in blankets and sheets of thick snow cast long looming shadows behind him, in the fiery orange sun. Jenson really wanted to make it to the hotel in time before sunset because he flat out didn't want to be driving in the dark.

Especially as he doubted there were street lights anywhere on his stretch of private road that supposedly led straight up to the English-owned hotel.

Jenson had known a lot of French and German people at university and if this private stretch of road was German-owned. Then it would be completely different and it would be impossible to die on the road.

That bought him little comfort as the Land Rover jerked and he could have sworn he screamed a little.

Jenson looked at his mum and dad who sat in the back to his right. They both looked identical in their long black coats, black hats and black thermal trousers.

They were smiling at him and his mum even held his hand but Jenson didn't mind. If he was going to die on some sort of private road with a sheer drop one side then he seriously wanted to be holding his mum's hand like a little kid.

Jenson looked up front next to the driver to see his older brother James smiling. Jenson wouldn't deny that James was just weird because apparently it was to hot to be wearing thermal clothes inside the car so he had taken off his clothes and was sitting in his shorts and t-shirt.

The madman.

Jenson wished it was warm but he was looking forward to the weekend away where he could relax, catch up with his family and just enjoy being somewhere different for a change. England was great and all but Jenson really did want a change.

"There storm coming tonight," the driver said with a minor French accent but it was hard to detect.

Jenson rolled his eyes. As much as he liked a good storm, he really liked watching storms window in the nice warm safety of his bedroom, he didn't like the idea of being stranded in the middle of nowhere in the middle of a massive storm.

"What do you mean storm?" Jenson's mother asked in perfect French.

Jenson smiled because he was glad his French lessons were finally paying off after all these years.

"There is eh, big snow storm coming," the driver said probably knowing he didn't need to try to be English anymore. "But it is eh, cool as you say. There are lots of shelter and people,"

Jenson was glad to hear it.

"And if you get trapped at eh… chalet, no. The

cabin then you will be rescued the next day or the next day after the storm stops,"

Jenson shook his head and spoke perfect French. "What if the storm doesn't stop for days?"

"Then as I said, you will eh, be rescued the day after,"

Jenson thanked him and admired the driver a lot for continuing to speak English even though he could have spoken French for all his family cared.

Jenson looked out over the wonderful mountain range and smiled as he saw the immense glass dome of the reception building. It dazzled, sparkled and shone so bright in the light of the setting sun, it looked almost magical.

Jenson turned around to his favourite brother, Nathan, who had his head stuck in a book about the Alps and carefully tapped his brother.

Nathan looked so small, tiny and still slightly like a teenage girl despite only starting on testosterone recently but Jenson really did love him. And it was so nice he had someone he could talk about hot boys with and it made Jenson smile even more as Nathan's face lit up at the sight of the hotel.

Then Nathan started looking all around the mountain range too. It wasn't exactly rare for him to be stuck in a book or learning about some weird and wonderful thing, it was why he was probably going to Oxford next year but Jenson was probably looking forward to spending more time with Nathan the most.

"We'll be at the hotel by the eh, time the storm comes in. And it will be massive," the driver said changing gears and Jenson just rolled his eyes.

He couldn't believe there was a good chance he was going to be snowed in with his whole family for a day or more and there was no chance of him escaping.

Jenson loved them more than he ever wanted to admit, but getting snowed-in with his family just wasn't his idea of fun.

He would even take getting snowed in with a hot guy at this point. At least that way he could actually *do* something or something productive during the storm.

Of course the guy would just abandon him after the holiday was over but that was life. It was what always happened to Jenson and his relationships.

But he would still love to experience a little holiday fun all whilst being snowed in. Anything to experience the thrill of *doing* a guy in the wonderful Alps.

And it wouldn't be until later Jenson realised he should have been a lot more careful about what he wished for.

CHAPTER 3
16th December 2023
The French Alps, France

As much as Carter flat out loved the wonderful mountain range, the hot hunk kissing his girlfriend outside and the great coffee he was enjoying, once the sun had dropped a little bit more, it was impossible for even him to stay outside.

Carter leant against a very warm white marble pillar at the very edge of the main domed reception area at the hotel, that he was fairly sure had a metal heating pipe running through it. Hence the heat. Even if he was wrong Carter was more than happy to wait here whilst the large red coach outside finished dropping off everyone.

The main reception area was as nice and huge as the rest of the hotel and the Alps. Carter really liked the warming black shiny flooring that was apparently made out of a special type of cinder block or another material that managed to capture the heat of the sun all day and it released the heat at night. It helped the hotel to keep their heating bills low.

And the entire hotel ran off very advance-looking solar panels that Carter had seen on the way to the hotel near the start of the private road.

The main reception desk was stunningly modern, beautiful and attractive with its seamless glass design that gave the entire reception a modern vibe that Carter really respected.

But Carter's favourite feature of the reception area had to be the golden chandelier. He had really liked the times him and his sister would talk about princesses, hot princes and what they would both have in their castles when they were older and their prince had rescued them. Carter had been firm that there would be chandeliers in every single room, so the very fact that he was seeing one now made him feel warm, special and hopeful that maybe his hot, hunkier prince would find him even after all these years.

Even the Christmas decorations from the red, blue and green tinsel wrapped around the pillars looked great and surprisingly enough worked seamlessly with the space. Carter really liked the immense Christmas tree in the middle of the reception area that just about touched the very bottom of the chandelier. The tree was filled with great-looking presents, Christmas crackers and so many other types of decorations that Carter was seriously starting to wonder if the hotel had caused a national decorations shortage in France.

There were certainly enough on the tree.

The first lot of tourists from the red coach started to come into the reception area. Carter smiled as the tourists shivered from the change in temperature as they took off their coats, gloves and goggles (why they were wearing them in the first place Carter didn't understand) so they could grab a hot drink before going back to their rooms.

Carter couldn't see his family yet.

His family had texted him that they could see the hotel and they would be back at any moment. He was so looking forward to seeing them and he really hoped that they had bought back some presents and gifts and food for him.

And if they hadn't, well now that his legs were feeling better after yesterday Carter was sure he would tickle and chase his big sister long enough until she surrendered some of her stuff to him. It had worked when they were kids so he didn't doubt it wouldn't work now.

"Carter!" his mother shouted.

Carter grinned like a little schoolboy as he saw his very tall and elegant mum, dad and big sister Katie come through the doors and quickly walk towards him.

Carter hugged his mum tight as she knocked the large paper bags of whatever rubbish she had bought.

"It was such a scary ride," his mum said. "There was an explosion, there were breakdowns and even the English were rioting in the village,"

Carter laughed and just looked at his sister, who was sort of the normal one in the family by all accounts.

She hugged Carter tight. "The coach backfired and it took three times to get it started. Then there was a massive argument in the town between an English couple and a French marketer who they were trying to steal from,"

Carter nodded. That made a lot more sense.

"But you would never guess who or, more like, what we found as we were getting off the coach," his mum said.

"And you smashed your bags into," Katie said.

Carter grinned as he felt like this was going to be good then he noticed his dad waving someone over.

"He's a gay man like you," his mum said.

Carter's stomach just tightened into a painful knot as he really didn't want this to be yet another crazy example of his mum's blind dating. And sheer inability to pick out attractive men.

"Um hi," a man said.

Carter looked at the direction of the voice and… well, well, well Carter had to admit his mum might have known how to pick men after all.

It took Carter a moment to really understand what he was looking at. He didn't know if the man was real, a delusion or maybe he was a demi-god or something.

Carter flat out loved the man's broad sexy

shoulders that even through his thick black coat told Carter that the hottie certainly worked out at the gym. Maybe four, five, seven times a week.

And Carter could just tell that the man had solid, long, sexy legs and a perfect stunning body under that coat. Seriously, Carter couldn't believe how much the coat was a crime against this hot hunk, it really did hide way too much of his sexy body.

The sexy body that Carter really, really wanted to explore later on.

But it was when Carter looked into the man's stunningly hot, intense emerald eyes that allowed him to see the Hunk's immense kindness, sexiness and sheer charming personality that he really fell for him. And the way the Hunk's short blond hair and wonderful smile framed his handsome face even more perfectly, if such a thing was possible, it seriously made Carter's wayward parts flare to life.

The Hunk was even hotter than the straight guy outside.

And that was when he immediately realised that he was in trouble. Because he didn't have a clue how he was going to be able to keep his hands to himself for his final night at the hotel.

Because all he wanted to do was touch, kiss and have sex with this demi-god amongst them. And he could only hope beyond hope that this sexy Hunk felt the exact same way.

CHAPTER 4
16th December 2023
The French Alps, France

After getting out of the Land Rover, after getting knocked into by an overdramatic middle-aged woman and after accidentally mentioning he was gay in a passing conversation with said woman, Jenson was really, really unsure of going into the massive domed hotel reception building.

He had to admit as he stood outside the immense glass doors with a constant flow of people to his right coming in from the same red coach that the woman, that seriously wanted him to mean her son, had come from. That the woman seemed nice enough and she seemed to really want him to meet her so-called attractive son, but Jenson had done this all before.

He had been on blind dates, he had kissed a lot of men he hadn't met before, that had ended up leaving him and abandoning him, but just for once he really did just want to meet a nice, wonderful man that didn't want to rush into anything.

"Jenson!" his mother shouted.

Jenson looked around and rolled his eyes as he saw that she was giving out the suitcases to everyone.

"Or," his father said, "you can go and do that nice thing that very nice young lady had suggested,"

Jenson laughed. He flat out loved his family, because it was basically a forced choice. He would pull a big heavy suitcase or go and meet a potentially very hot man who he could have passionate sex with, after getting to know him, of course.

Jenson went in through the immense glass doors and shivered at the sheer temperature difference between outside and the wonderful reception area. He had imagined a few little Christmas decorations but this was unreal.

The huge Christmas tree covered in blue, green and red tinsel took up the entire middle of the black marble floor. It looked so stunning, beautiful and the way sweet Christmas music played in the background was really heartwarming.

Jenson was so glad he had come here. The entire reception area smelt of rich warming spices, mince pies and more than enough mulled wine that Jenson was fairly sure if he spent too long here he might actually get hungover.

It was perfect.

"Jenson darling," he heard someone say.

Jenson looked over in the direction of the sound to see the bat-crap crazy woman that had smashed into him earlier and presumably her husband were waving at him. And Jenson supposed he really did have to go and see them because otherwise he would be stuck pulling suitcases.

He really didn't want to do that. Not when he had watched his mother pack them and he had even joked about adding the kitchen sink to the cases. Only to have to fight the kitchen sink in his mother's hands so she didn't add it.

Those suitcases were going to be as heavy as an elephant. If not more so.

Jenson went over to the scary woman and her husband.

And that's when he noticed the most beautiful, smiley, drop-dead gorgeous man he had ever had the privilege of seeing.

His ability to speak died. He stumbled a little. His heart pounded in his chest like an earthquake.

And he forced himself not to fall over and die from the sheer shock of finding such a divinely beautiful man so high up in the Alps.

Jenson just couldn't help but focus on the thin hoody, trousers and snow boots the sexy man was wearing. They highlighted his fit, slightly muscular body that Jenson really wanted to touch, admire and kiss. His body looked so tender, soft and smooth that Jenson wanted to look away before his wayward parts flared to life but he couldn't.

The man was too beautiful to look away from.

Jenson couldn't believe how angular and model-like the man's wonderful face was. He easily could have modelled for all the top fashion magazines if he really wanted to, and the way his stunning, slightly long brown hair was parted to one side, it only enhanced his sheer beauty.

There wasn't a single thing wrong with this stunning man.

Jenson realised he had stopped walking so he forced himself to keep going towards them. The only problem was the closer he got to the stunning man the harder it was to walk.

His legs were freezing up, his breathing was more like panting at this point and his throat was beyond dry.

He couldn't believe he was having such a strong reaction to a stranger, but the man was the most beautiful man he had ever seen.

"Um, hi," Jenson said forcing out each word.

He loved it when the stunning man looked at him and grinned like a little schoolboy. Jenson really hoped he found him as attractive as Jenson found him.

He wanted to look at the parents and the other woman that was with them but he didn't want to stop looking at the stunning man, not even for a second.

"Well say something then," the woman said to her son.

"Hey,"

Jenson laughed and went a little closer to him. He was so glad he wasn't the only one that was finding talking hard.

"This is the man I told you about. The man that tried to tackle me to the ground,"

Jenson just looked at the woman but thankfully the younger woman, maybe her daughter, came over and hugged Jenson a little.

"Relax," she said. "My mother likes to overexaggerate," then she turned to her brother. "Mum rammed her suitcase into the poor sod,"

Jenson smiled. He had a feeling he was really going to like getting to know this family and he had a little feeling that the stunning man's mother and father wasn't exactly going to let the idea of him and their son together go away any time soon.

And Jenson didn't have a problem at all with that.

Not a problem at all.

CHAPTER 5
16th December 2023
The French Alps, France

As much as Carter flat out loved his mother on this one occasion for her so-called match-making abilities, he really had no idea why they had basically hounded the poor Hunk's parents and family about joining them for an evening drink after they were checked in.

It definitely wasn't that Carter did not want to spend more time with the gorgeous Hunk but he wanted to do it in private, so they could talk, they could talk about gay stuff, life and maybe even kiss a little without having to make their families watch it.

Carter had decided that if he was going to be meeting the Hunk (and hopefully finding out his name) and his family, then he wanted to meet them all somewhere that wasn't icy cold. Meaning he sadly couldn't go outside but he certainly wanted to try taking the Hunk out there later on.

Instead Carter was currently sitting on a very comfortable brown fabric sofa with an empty space for the Hunk to his left and Katie on his right. Then his parents sat on another sofa opposite him with there being another two armchairs in-between the sofas.

Carter wanted to rest his feet up on the large glass coffee table in the middle of them but he couldn't do that now his parents were here. And he didn't want the Hunk or his parents to think he wasn't "domestically trained" or whatever rubbish term his mother used in the past to basically say that they weren't chavy.

There it was again the English and their snobbiness.

Carter leant forward and picked up the massive mug of creamy piping hot hot chocolate that his mother had got him, and he was the only one not drinking as everyone else had gotten themselves a mulled wine. Carter really didn't like to drink but he couldn't deny the mulled wine smelt great.

"What did you get today?" Carter asked his mother, really hoping there were no over-the-top stories.

"Well funny you should mention that," his mum asked. "Because there was a beautiful glass bowl dating back from the 1800s in the town market so I asked the man how much. And he said twenty euros, now you know me I love a good bargain so I bought it instantly,"

Carter looked at Katie. "Let me guess mass produced rubbish from China last year?"

Katie smiled and nodded. Carter really did love his mum, she definitely never failed to make him smile, and worried about her and her wild ideas at times.

"Hi," a short man said with a high-pitched voice who sort of had an air and look of a teenage girl around him as he gestured if he sat down on the armchair.

Carter nodded as he recognised the short man from the Hunk's family earlier at the check-in.

"I'm Nathan and my family will be over in a moment," he said placing a book on the Alps down on the table along with a Diet Coke.

"Aren't you cold enough for a Diet Coke?" Carter asked kindly.

"Of course not," Nathan said. "You can never be too cold for a coke,"

Carter nodded. "True to that,"

Carter grinned as he noticed the fit, beautiful muscular Hunk was here with his parents and other brother. Carter was so glad the Hunk sat next to him and because he had accidentally chosen a sofa that was a little small for three people, Carter just had to wrap his arm around the fit sexy Hunk.

Carter flat out loved the wonderful hardness of the Hunk's body as he grinned like a little schoolboy. And his entire body shook with attraction, pleasure and passion.

He never wanted to let go of the sexy hunk's body.

"I'm Jenson," the Hunk said.

"Carter," he said shaking the man's hand with his left so it was a little weird but he was shocked by the strength, grip and attraction in the handshake.

"How long are you here for?" Jenson's mother asked.

"One more night sadly," Carter said.

"Why sadly?" Jenson's oldest brother asked with an evil grin.

Carter really didn't like being put on the spot but he had a feeling that if a grown man was silly enough to wear shorts in the Alps, then he was probably wanting to embarrass Carter.

"Is it because you want to talk to and fuck by younger brother?"

"James," Jenson said. "That is rude, uncalled for and whatever happens between me and this... very attractive man is none of your business,"

Carter grinned and went so close to the hot man's ear that he really liked feeling Jenson's body warm against his. "So you find me attractive?"

Jenson nodded clearly embarrassed.

"How about we go somewhere?" Carter asked then he realised he sounded a little much so he pulled back a little so everyone could hear them. "So we can just get to know each other. That's all I promise,"

"Are you going on the decking area?" his mother asked.

Carter nodded, really hoping she wasn't about to go into another wild story.

"Well you be careful beautifuls. First time I went out there it was blowing so much I almost flew off the decking and fell to my death," his mother said.

Carter gestured to wonderful Jenson they really needed to go now unless they wanted to be trapped here forever listening to one crazy story after another.

"How would that work?" Nathan asked like the story might actually be true.

And Carter loved it when his mother's eyes lid up at knowing someone wanted to listen to her for a change. Carter had a feeling that the two families were going to get on perfectly and now he only wanted to spend some nice quality time with a wonderfully beautiful man.

Something that seriously wasn't helped by Katie smacking his ass as he guided Jenson outside.

CHAPTER 6
16th December 2023
The French Alps, France

Jenson was flat out amazed at how dark it was already outside despite the light from the moon, as he held Carter's wonderfully soft, smooth hand as he led them out onto the decking area. He was really impressed with how large the brown decking area was, the brown sofas looked so inviting and cozy and all he wanted to do was simply settle down with Carter in one and just talk.

He didn't want to kiss, hug or have sex with Carter. He felt something deeper and more personal with Carter because he was clearly a nice guy and it was clear he came from a great family.

Sure Carter's family seemed a little weird but it was great to see how much they all loved each other. And Carter's family had to be great if Nathan was talking instead of reading something, he never ever did that no matter how much his parents pushed him.

Jenson shivered a little and pulled Carter a little closer but they were both wearing such thick coats that he sadly couldn't feel Carter's body warmth. He had loved sitting next to him on the sofa because it was so nice having a guy wrap his arm around him without expecting anything in return.

This had just been a perfect evening so far.

Carter pointed over to the edge of the decking area and Jenson really didn't want to go over there. The large metal railings were all lit up in red, green and copper Christmas lights but he was only realising now he had a minor fear of heights.

He followed sexy Carter over to the edge of the decking area and he felt like such an ant as he stared out into the sheer darkness of the Alps below him.

The entire mountain range seemed so magical as he might as well have been wearing sunglasses. He could still clearly see the outline of each and every mountain in such perfect detail because of the pure whiteness of the snow reflected the moonlight so perfectly.

There thankfully wasn't much of a wind and the sheer silence of the decking area was so nice, romantic and stunning that all Jenson wanted to do in that moment was kiss the beautiful lips of the man next to him.

But he forced himself not to.

"Your family seem nice," Jenson said knowing it was the only thing he could think of.

"Thanks and they really are. They love you by the

way," Carter said knowing he was just saying the only think he could think of. "And it's nice that my mum and Nathan are getting on,"

"My parents are going to be over the moon about that," Jenson said. "Nathan's normally really bookish and quiet and he tends to avoid people like the plague. He only really talks to me for the fun of it, so we talk about boys, how he's coping and everyone else,"

Carter leant on the railings and Jenson just shook his head. He so wasn't brave enough to do that. What if the railings broke from the cold?

"What do you mean *coping?* If you don't mind me asking. He seems like a great kid, I don't know why people wouldn't like him,"

That only made Jenson like him even more. Carter was hot, a good judge of character and he wasn't judgemental. Jenson really didn't know if there could be anything wrong with Carter.

"He hasn't exactly had an easy few years because he always liked guys which was fine. But he's, trans so that didn't cause any problems in the family but at school. Let's just say kids can be mean,"

Carter just nodded. "He looks great,"

Jenson laughed. Of course Jenson wouldn't judge, be mean or react negatively because Carter really was a perfect guy that was really hot too.

"Being trans is normal as far as I care," Carter said. "How long are you here for anyway?"

Jenson laughed. "Just the weekend and then we

leave the resort Monday. It's a shame you're only here for a single night. Maybe the storm will change that,"

"Hopefully," Carter said grinning. "But it is really beautiful here with the Christmas lights, the snow covered peaks and the great company,"

Jenson gently forced himself to lean against the icy coldness of the metal railings, and now he was just paranoid about getting stuck to them. He was so damn relieved that the railings were breaking or making a sound but he heard Carter laugh next to him.

"You really aren't a natural at heights are you?" Carter asked.

"I am a complete natural," Jenson said wanting Carter to think he wasn't scared of anything.

"You are scared and that's okay," Carter said knowing he was trying to be fearless for some reason. "And I think a little fear makes a guy even hotter because it means he's real and not a fake,"

Jenson grinned. "Well then Mr Carter, I am very, very scared. So scared in fact you might need to hold me,"

Carter laughed and fell against Jenson's chest and Jenson gently kissed him on the head. It wasn't that romantic as they were both wearing so many clothes and kissing a thick fake fur hat wasn't that great, but Jenson loved feeling Carter's laughter vibrate through him.

This was going to be an amazing weekend and maybe the storm could buy them some extra, precious time together.

"Men we are closing the decking area now because of the storm," a woman from the hotel said.

Jenson took Carter's hand in his and they both hurried into the warmth and now Jenson just wondered if and how he was going to get the chance to kiss Carter again.

Something he wanted to do far more than he had any right to want.

CHAPTER 7
16th December 2023
The French Alps, France

Carter was so glad his mum and dad and Katie were already two steps ahead of him as they had already arranged for the two families to have dinner together. He had to admit this was all moving way too fast for his liking but it was brilliant that their families were getting on like a house on fire. Even Katie and James seemed to be hitting it off in more ways than one.

To Carter's utter dismay.

Carter really liked the slight warmth coming from the black wooden chairs as he sat at the head of the table with sexy Jenson to his left and Nathan to his right. The massively long glass dining table was the perfect size for all of them and Carter was so glad to see all the smiling, laughing and talking between everyone.

And he actually believed for a moment that this

hadn't been the first time they had all met. Maybe they had met before on another holiday, another time or another place because everyone felt like they had all been friends for decades.

Carter wrapped his hands around the wonderfully warm mug of English breakfast tea, because he was getting to have enough of coffee and hot chocolate (words he thought he would never ever have say) and he couldn't help but stare into Jenson's beautiful emerald eyes.

"How's the skiing here?" Jenson asked.

"It's really good actually," Carter said not wanting to tell Jenson about his competitiveness with Katie yesterday. "It's a lot of fun. What brand is your gear?"

Jenson frowned a little and looked at Nathan.

Nathan put down the new book he was reading on geo-thermal energy. "We didn't bring any gear because parents wanted to rent it off the holiday,"

"Oh," Carter said not wanting to come off as snobbish. "You must come and see our gear later on because it's good, effective and you might as well use it when we go,"

"But don't you want to keep it and use it again," Jenson said liking his slight snobbishness. "I mean you did have to pay for it all,"

"I think what he means is," Nathan said, "if you have the gear then he has to come and see you again,"

Carter really liked Nathan. He was as sharp as anyone sitting at the table and he really, really hoped

Nathan was going to go far in life.

"Where do you come from actually?" Carter asked.

"We come from Kent. Dover to be more precise in the South of England. Have you heard of it?" Jenson asked.

Carter nodded. "Of course I have. We come from Sussex so just the county over. Nice, it wouldn't be that hard to get to you,"

Carter loved it when Jenson blushed and looked really flushed. He didn't know why but there was just something about Jenson, the way he acted, how kind he was and just everything about him that Carter liked him more and more.

"Tell him what you do," Nathan said pretending to say it quietly but failing.

"Your little brother wants you to know I just finished my Masters in Clinical Psychology,"

"Oh cool," Carter said. "I started my Masters back in September, and psychology no less, very nice. What mental health population do you want to work with?"

Carter liked it as Nathan dropped the book he was reading and Jenson's beautiful mouth dropped open.

"Um, I want to work with working-aged adults mostly specialising in trans people," Jenson said. "So I can support their mental health during the traumatic time and I can help diagnose them with gender dysphoria and they can start transitioning sooner,"

Carter was impressed, and it was great how Jenson wanted to use his degree to help people like his brother. A group that Carter supposed not a lot of mental health workers wanted or were able to support as much as they needed.

"But jobs with that population are few and far between so I'm currently working as an Assistant Psychologist in a hospital with people with depression and anxiety,"

Carter nodded. There wasn't really a lot he could say because this wasn't his area of interest at all, but it was nice seeing the light, fire and passion in Jenson's eyes about his subject and his work and what he wanted to do with his future.

"How did you know clinical psychologists work with different populations or clinical settings?" Jenson asked.

Carter smiled. "I used to have a boyfriend that studied psychology and wanted to work in the NHS. You might know him, Aden Lee,"

"Oh. Yeah I know Aden Lee, the man with the weird birthmark on his ass,"

Carter just smiled and he supposed he shouldn't have been surprised that Jenson had slept or at least *done* Aden. Even when him and Aden were going out Aden seemed to be a player and into every single guy that moved.

He wouldn't have been surprised if Aden had only dated him to get access to some "fresh blood" outside the School of Psychology.

Carter was about to ask another Aden question but then the plates of rich, sticky garlic doughballs for their starters came out and Carter was seriously looking forward to them.

He was starving and flat out looking forward to spending even more time with such a wonderful man.

CHAPTER 8
16th December 2023
The French Alps, France

Jenson flat out couldn't remember the last time he had been this relaxed, this happy and this excited about having dinner with an insanely hot man in his life. Everything about today had been so great that Jenson had wanted to pinch himself just in case this was a dream.

Thankfully after he spilled boiling hot tea on his manly area he certainly knew this wasn't a dream.

Jenson was surprised how great, Christmassy and colourful the dining area was with the red, blue and copper tinsel wrapped around the stunning chandeliers and light fixtures. And the Christmas music playing in the background added such warmth, coziness and love to the dining experience that Jenson was in his element.

He had to admit that he was a little unsure about Katie and James getting on so well, because he really wasn't sure what James would be like. He didn't want Katie to get hurt by his brother but he hadn't seen James smile and laugh so much in a long time. It was almost like he was a totally different person because of Katie.

Katie being a witch was the only conclusion Jenson could come to explain all of it.

"How's the food?" a man asked as he came over to the table.

Jenson was seriously enjoying the incredibly rich, buttery doughballs that melted on his tongue unleashing a great explosion of mellow garlicy goodness in his mouth. If all the food tasted like this then Jenson would be shocked if he didn't gain tons of weight over the next week.

The food was sensational.

"So Nathan," Carter said, "what got you interested in reading?"

As Jenson watched Carter and Nathan talk, laugh and debate some of the various topics he had been reading up on, Jenson had to admit he was really falling for Carter.

They might have only met four, five hours ago but it was amazing how perfectly and naturally he seemed to bond with his family. All he had ever wanted to be honest was a boyfriend that could get on with his family, love them all and never react badly to Nathan being trans.

Something even a lot of gay people were still unsure about, but not Carter. Carter was just a hot, sexy, kind person that Jenson was certain could do no wrong whatsoever.

"You should take your big brother skiing at some point and show him all those cool moves you've read about," Carter said and Jenson liked seeing Nathan's eyes light up.

Something Jenson was only realising he hadn't seen for ages.

Jenson didn't know why but he looked outside through the immense triple-glazed floor-to-ceiling windows of the dining area and was surprised to see how heavy the snow was falling outside.

It was so heavy that the snow had already moved up a good few inches at the bottom of the windows. It hadn't been like that only moments before.

"I hope we get dessert before they send us back to our rooms," Carter said.

"I don't know. I think I'm looking at my dessert," Jenson said grinning.

"Oh no," Carter's mother said and Jenson just rolled his eyes. If anyone could make a little dusting of snow into a horror story it would certainly be his future mother-in-law.

Jenson was actually wondering how she would tell her friends about how him and Carter met. Would there be a snow monster? An evil criminal? Or just some other crazy random story that would take hold in Carter's mother's weird and vivid imagination.

"We better get back to the cabin and unpack," his mother said.

Jenson looked at Carter and he leant closer to the man he was really, really liking. "You know if we go back to your cabin together, we can keep each other warm tonight,"

"And who knows how long the storm will last?" Carter asked grinning like a teenage boy.

"Lucky," Nathan said shaking his head.

"I'm sure there's another gay guy in the hotel for you little bro," Jenson said staring into Carter's wonderfully soft eyes.

"Ladies and Gentlemen," a very tall woman said as she came in with a small team of hotel staff. "Because the storm is coming up earlier than expected we have suspended the dinner service. Earlier today we added extra water, food and heaters in your cabins,"

Jenson rolled his eyes. This was his worst nightmare. He was flat out not staying in a cabin with his family for God knows how long.

"Please return to your cabins because they will be warmer than the main reception building. But before you go please tell one of my staff members exactly where you will be tonight for the storm. We need to know in case someone gets lost,"

Jenson held Carter's hand out of instinct and he loved how great, right and natural it felt. He really didn't want to get lost in a snowstorm of all things.

"Lovers," Jenson's mother said. "How about if Jenson and Carter come with us for the night? Then James and Katie can go back to yours,"

"Actually," Jenson shouted by mistake. "Can we swap?"

"Are you shamed of us?" Jenson's father asked with a grin.

"Generally yes," Jenson said forcing himself not to laugh. "But on this occasion I don't want to spend a snowstorm with you,"

"Feeling's mutual," Jenson's family said as one and they all laughed.

Then Jenson hugged everyone at the table, told James to behave himself and wished Katie a hell of a lot of luck and then he followed Carter and his parents back to their cabin holding the smooth, soft hand of the man he was seriously falling for.

CHAPTER 9
16th December 2023
The French Alps, France

As Carter led sexy, hunky Jenson into his log cabin that had been his home for the past week, he was really impressed with Jenson's reaction. His beautiful mouth dropped and he just seemed stunned.

Carter really knew the feeling as he shut and locked the door behind them. Every single time he walked in here he was still amazed by the sheer beauty of it all.

The entire log cabin was a wonderful design of a single massive living room with sofas, throws and blankets with the great-looking focal point being the huge fireplace set against one of the log walls. Even the workmanship was impressive as hell to Carter as he ran his fingers across the perfectly smooth walls near the door. He didn't know why he did it but it seemed to make Jenson smile.

His parents were already going into the back of

the cabin where all the very small and cozy bedrooms were. He supposed the bedrooms were so small to keep the heat in and Carter was so looking forward to taking Jenson into his later on. It would be so cosy, romantic and alluring that Carter was certain they would be kissing in no time.

And that was hardly a bad thing.

It was even more beautiful with all the immense rows upon rows of red, blue and green tinsel so stylishly wrapped around the lights, and artfully stuck in-between the huge logs themselves. Carter really liked the Christmas tree too but that was when his Dad caught his eye.

"What your poison?" Carter's dad asked Jenson as he came back into the living room holding two large bottles of wine. One was white, one was red.

Then his mother came in with another two bottles of whiskey. Carter should have known that his parents would stock up on alcohol.

"Is it really a good idea to be drinking when we could freeze to death?" Jenson asked. "Considering alcohol makes you feel warm when your body temperature is dropping,"

Carter supposed that was a good point but he still took Jenson by the hand and pulled him over to the sofa next to the one his parents were sitting at.

He was glad Jenson took the initiative by sitting down and pulling him on top of him. Carter loved feeling Jenson's hard body under him and he just loved they were going to be spending the night together.

Even if it was their only night together.

"That is true but I would rather die drunk and warm than sober and cold," his father said.

Carter laughed and pulled Jenson's strong arms round him like a blanket.

"Do you think our daughter's okay with your brother?" Carter's dad asked.

Carter was surprised Jenson didn't answer for a moment.

"I normally would say no and that I was concerned about your daughter getting hurt. But from what I've seen tonight, your daughter is just as strong and capable and able to handle herself as your son. You've both clearly done a great job,"

Carter hugged Jenson a little more but frowned when his mother smiled like she had another story.

"I like this one. He is so much nicer and better than your old boyfriend. What was his name? Oh yes, Stephen O'Claire,"

"Oh god that idiot," his father said.

Carter really wished his parents would be quiet but his throat was too dry to talk.

"So one night Carter deary," his mother said, "went to the pub with the lads from uni. It was literally raining cats and dogs and we thought he was going to drown and die,"

In all fairness Carter couldn't deny he might have died that night, just not from the rain, and more like the sheer amount of alcohol he drank.

"Then the next morning he woke up and found Carter in sleep with this chavy guy he picked up. They tried dating for a single day and Stephen was smelly, swearing and he vomited all over Carter,"

Carter sat up a little and shook his head at Jenson. "Don't get any ideas. It was disgusting,"

He loved hearing Jenson laugh more and more as he imagined what that was like so Carter got up and lit the pre-made fire that the hotel staff had been nice enough to make. There were tons of logs either side of the fire and it was all locally sourced and it was certified the tree farm was managed as environmentally friendly as it possibly could be. And for every tree cut down another was planted in its place.

Carter loved that about the hotel.

The living room thankfully didn't take that long to warm up so he snuggled back into Jenson's wonderfully hard body as his parents poured themselves a drink.

"Are you sure you don't want one?" his father asked.

Carter smiled and shook his head. He hadn't drunk for the last twenty-something years, he certainly didn't need to start drinking now.

The log roof creaked a little and Carter looked outside through the surprisingly thick windows and frowned when he could only see whiteness.

The storm had already caused enough snow to fall so the windows were covered and Carter was really concerned with just how much snow would fall.

And he had no idea how long it could take them to get out of the cabin when it eventually stopped but with his parents and sexy Jenson by his side he really wasn't that worried.

Because two horny young men could find a lot of ways to kill the time.

"Let's play a board game," Carter's father said and Carter just laughed. He really did love his family and Jenson a lot more than he ever wanted to admit.

CHAPTER 10
16th August 2023
The French Alps, France

After playing five rounds of Connect 4, playing even more rounds of draughts and even beating sexy Carter at chess three times, Jenson really did love listening to the gentle snoring of Carter's parents after drinking too much and he was really impressed their snoring was perfectly in tune with the Christmas songs gently playing in the background.

Jenson didn't *actually* like their snoring because he wasn't a creep and he didn't like watching older people sleep, that was just flat out weird. But he really liked it because it meant that him and sexy Carter were completely alone on the sofa together.

Jenson ran his fingers through Carter's wonderful short hair and he liked listening to Carter's soft and shallow breathing. He might have been a little tired himself but Jenson was really enjoying his time with him in the cabin.

The cabin itself was stunning and the Christmas decorations were a lot more than he was expecting. Especially the massive fir in one corner of the cabin. He had never seen so many lights, stars and other weird, more traditional decorations hanging off a tree in all his life.

It was beautiful, if not a little over-the-top.

"Why did your family want to come here so close to Christmas?" Jenson asked.

"A catch-up really," Carter said. "I haven't seen them a lot and they just wanted to have some fun together before me and my sister move out, get our own lives and that sort of thing gets a lot harder,"

Jenson nodded and he gently ran his finger down Carter's nice, hard body. He didn't have any muscles or anything but his body was nice, firm and Jenson really wanted to keep touching it.

The howling, roaring wind outside made Jenson shake his head as soon as he noticed the window was completely white now. It was impossible to see out of it so Jenson knew that they were well and truly snowed in.

There was no chance of escape until tomorrow and that was only if the snow stopped.

"Have you ever fantasized about being snowed in?" Jenson asked grinning and just curious about what happened inside Carter's pretty little head.

"Actually I have a range of fantasies with hot men," Carter said wanting to satisfy his curiosity. "I have a fantasy about a prince saving me and fucking me. I have another fantasy about just finding a man that loved me for me. And my favourite fantasy involves us going into the bedroom right now,"

"If you two are gonna do that then please keep it down," Carter's mother said as she drifted off back to sleep.

Jenson laughed into Carter's coconut-scented hair and kissed it. All Jenson wanted to do was kiss, hug and do so many amazing things to Carter that it would be a night they would remember forever long after tonight.

Carter stood up, took Jenson by the hand and led himself to his bedroom.

Jenson had no idea what to expect but he was so nervous, so unsure of himself and he really forced his leg to move.

What if he was bad? What if Carter had had better sex? What if everything? Jenson couldn't believe how nervous Carter made him about someone he was normally very, very good at.

At least according to other men.

Jenson smiled as Carter led him into his little log cabin bedroom. It was hardly massive, it was barely large enough for a single bed, desk and two chairs. He really didn't mind sharing a small bed with Carter because that was critical for body warmth.

Carter went over to the bed and took off his top. Jenson grinned like a little teenage boy that had never seen another guy topless before.

Jenson just couldn't help but admire Carter's fit

body. He had never expected him to be *that* fit with the very faint outline of a six-pack, pecs and everything else that he loved in a man.

Carter came over to him. And kissed.

It was quick and promising of something more to come but Jenson still loved it. It was loving, passionate and tender. It was everything Jenson had ever wanted in a kiss.

And now all he wanted was Carter. And his body. And everything about Carter.

Jenson shut and locked the door behind him and then he made passionate love to the man he seriously falling for.

CHAPTER 11
16th December 2023
The French Alps, France

About an hour later, Carter just grinned as he rested his back against the slightly warm headboard of the bed while Jenson started to drift off to sleep.

Carter flat out couldn't believe how great, intense and amazing the sex had been. He had had more than enough sex with other men before, but there was just something else, something deeper, something more personal about having sex with Jenson.

It was like all the other sex in his life he had had was nothing compared to the sheer passion and intensity that Jenson had given him. And it also helped that he was amazing at it too, so much so Carter had barely had to do any of the work.

That was always a massive bonus.

Carter listened to the howling, roaring and whipping of the snowstorm outside, but it was muffled slightly because of the sheer thickness of the snow around the cabin. He didn't mind it, he knew that his mum and dad were a little nervous but the French were very practical and passionate people.

If they wanted to get something done then they would do it, or burn it down. Either way they would get rescued and then Carter realised what that meant.

Carter looked down at the beautifully loving, passionate and naked man he was really starting to fall for. Jenson was snoring lightly and when they were rescued, Carter would have to go home with family and that meant not seeing Jenson.

Sure they only lived one county over but it wasn't the same. It would require doing things long distance and that was hard and they both had lives outside of each other and this relationship.

And it was a relationship.

Carter had had holiday flings before, he had loved them and he had fucked at least three men for fun whilst on family holidays. That was okay and he enjoyed them, but they all felt the same.

This did not feel like a holiday fling in the slightest.

This felt passionate, intense and loving, and it didn't matter they had only met each other a few hours before because that was the magical thing about being in France, the country of love, and being trapped together in a snowstorm. It really did clarify things for Carter.

And he knew without a shadow of a doubt that he wanted Jenson and Jenson wanted him.

"You look intense," Jenson said as Carter noticed he was looking at him. Jenson looked so cute.

"Just thinking about what happens when we go back," Carter said. "I'm meant to leave tomorrow and then we'll be apart,"

"I do want a relationship," Jenson said more forcefully than he probably meant.

Carter ran his fingers through his wonderfully short blond hair. "Me too but… I don't know how it would work,"

"Does anyone know how long-distance relationships work? And I mean is it really that long distance, it's a county apart,"

"Do you drive?" Carter asked. "I don't,"

"Well no but you know what English public transport is like," Jenson said.

Carter laughed. Everyone in England knew exactly how awful, chaotic and useless public transport was, unlike in Scotland where it was a hell of a lot better.

"We'll make it work," Carter said knowing he really wasn't sure about that.

"The storm," Jenson said frowning.

Carter listened for a moment. At first he could only hear the sexy breathing of Jenson, the man he really liked, but then he realised that the howling, roaring wind was gone.

And so was the storm.

"We'll be rescued tomorrow," Jenson said.

Carter felt his voice wobble and his throat went

dry. This was their final night, their final night of being together because they would be rescued tomorrow and then his family would have to go to the airport.

And leave Jenson behind for at least a week. But what if Jenson didn't care about him after a week apart so when he returned to the UK he never contacted him?

Carter hated the idea as his stomach twisted into a painful knot.

So he snuggled into bed with the man he never wanted to lose and then he kissed Jenson on the lips just in case their number of kisses they gave each other were coming to an end.

The very thing that scared Carter the most.

CHAPTER 12
17th December 2023
The French Alps, France

Jenson had no idea that it was 8 am in the morning despite that his phone had told him that. The windows were still blacked out by the snow, the wind was thankfully gone and all the beautiful Christmas lights lit up the living room wonderfully.

He really did love the cabin and he was so looking forward to spending the next week in his own one with his family. It would have been so much better if Carter was there with him but that was life. And they would certainly meet up back in the UK, Jenson was going to move heaven and Earth to make sure that happened.

And he was even going to start looking for Assistant Psychologist jobs in Sussex in case there was a chance he would move down there in a few months' time. He didn't know why he wanted to wait a few months, his love for Carter was a sure thing and it was so much more intense, great and loving than he had ever felt before.

Carter was the most beautiful man he had ever met and he never wanted to be a part from him.

When Jenson went into the living room, he smiled at Carter's Mum as she was cooking them all a big breakfast of sausages, bacon and eggs. It all smelt great and Jenson was so looking forward to spending time with Carter and his family over breakfast.

He went over to the long kitchen island she was standing behind and he sat there. Jenson did want to help but Carter's Mum seemed more than able.

"Where's our favourite man?" Carter's Mum asked.

"In bed," Jenson said, "he wanted to stay in a little longer. I think he's worried about you leaving today and he might think I'll leave him after I return to the UK,"

"Would you?"

Jenson laughed. "Of course not. Carter's a brilliant man and I really, really like him,"

"Well I hate to burst your loving bubble but I got an email this morning,"

Jenson's stomach sank like a stone at the words. He knew this was going to be extremely bad, awful and things couldn't be worse for their relationship.

"Did Carter ever tell you how he wanted to move to Scotland for his Masters?"

Jenson shrugged. He couldn't blame Carter at all. Scotland was a beautiful country, very positive and it was the best country in the entire UK regardless of what the UK Government told people with their lies.

"Well he didn't get into a bunch of universities but he always wanted to study in Edinburgh and some places have opened up. The University said they would be happy to work with him to see what modules he's already done and they want him,"

Jenson nodded. It was all he could do.

Jenson jumped as he felt too massive arms wrap around him and Carter kissed his neck slowly.

And then his Mum told him about the email.

"Brilliant," Carter said. "That is going to be amazing. It's the university of my dreams,"

Jenson just nodded. There was nothing else he could do. He was more than happy for their relationship to be distanced by a County, but an entire country. That was a bit different.

"Why do just stay at your current university?" Jenson asked trying not to sound too judgmental.

"Because I have always wanted to study in Scotland. It is UK-leading for education and Scotland is world-renowned for their lecturers and universities. And I love the country, the culture, the politics. I love it all," Carter said.

Jenson smiled. It was great to see how happy, passionate and excited Carter was. He honestly looked the happiest he had been since last night.

He realised how happy he made Carter. Carter's smile that reached his eyes about his great opportunity was the same as he had had ever since they had met yesterday.

But Jenson really didn't know where this left their relationship. He had a job, he had a life, he had friends down in Kent in England. He couldn't move to Scotland no matter how much better it was than England.

"What's going to happen to us?" Jenson asked.

"We'll make it work. We'll be together. And we'll visit each other whenever we can," Carter said hugging Jenson as tight as he could.

Jenson grinned because he believed Carter with all his heart. He was just unsure about himself, could he deal with a long-distance relationship and if not was it fair on Carter not to tell him how he felt.

Jenson knew as he had *done* Carter last night and they had kissed, hugged and made extremely hot love, he never ever realised Carter could be the same as all the other guys before him. Just man that said he really liked him but ultimately Carter was just going to leave him.

Maybe there was hope, just a little hope. Yet Jenson still wasn't sure if he could handle a very long-distance relationship. It seemed impossible.

He had until the end of breakfast to figure that out.

Or maybe less as everyone jumped at the sound of shovels banging into the front door.

They were rescued.

CHAPTER 13
17th December 2023
The French Alps, France

After talking to the brave men and women at the hotel who had shovelled should tons of snow since first light in an effort to save as many people as possible, Carter really liked the incredibly crispy bacon, juicy apple and onion sausages and egg that his Mum had made for them.

He was so excited about going back to the UK now. He had a bunch of paperwork to fill out and then they needed to finalise on-campus accommodation details and he was so excited about starting, or more like finishing off his Masters, in the city of his dreams.

Carter had completely forgotten he had even applied to Edinburgh before his Mum had mentioned it. but it was a great university, a great Masters programme and it was a really, really beautiful city.

Granted it wasn't anywhere near as beautiful as

Jenson but they would visit each other, call daily and Carter would come down whenever he could. He was never going to let their relationship die just because he wanted to study in the city of his dreams.

Carter grinned at the wonderful man he loved and he realised that Jenson was being a lot quieter than normal.

"The coach is picking us up at midday," his Mum said. "So make sure you're packed by 10 then we can sit in the Main Building and have a final coffee and chat with Jenson and his family if you want,"

Carter nodded. He would love that. It didn't give him long to pack up but it wouldn't take that long.

Carter smiled at Jenson and again he wasn't talking.

"I won't leave you, you know?" Carter asked. "I really like you and we will make the long-distance thing work,"

Jenson nodded, but Carter could tell that he was being passive-aggressive as hell.

"What?" Carter asked trying and failing to stop a hint of anger getting in his voice.

"I just don't know if *I* can do a long-distance relationship,"

Carter sliced up the last juicy sausage on his plate and he nodded. He wanted to at least seem respectful to Jenson but all Carter wanted to do was tell him that together they could do anything together.

"Why not?" Carter's Dad asked.

Jenson moved uncomfortably. "Because what if

we grow apart, what if we both need love and the other is busy. Will we actually stay in contact or only say that?"

Carter wasn't sure where all this fear was coming from. They had just spent the past day together having fun, making memories and enjoying each other's time like they had been boyfriends for years.

"You know we'll call, text and video chat tons. You know me," Carter said.

"No. No I don't," Jenson said. "I met you less than a day ago and I can't know anything about you. And come on, you deserve to be free when you move. You can find a nice boy you can sleep with, talk to and go out with. I don't want to drag you down,"

Carter just laughed and shook his head. He had to be joking. This was the biggest load of shit he had ever heard.

"Goodbye Carter," Jenson said getting up from the table and he went to hug Carter but he moved away.

Carter was not letting Jenson touch him after dumping him.

Carter just watched Jenson walk away. He couldn't speak, he couldn't think, he couldn't do anything.

His entire world was falling down around him because it wasn't even like there was a snowstorm anymore.

CHAPTER 14
17th December 2023
The French Alps

Jenson was rather surprised that his family, Katie and James had all been rescued before him and Carter were so they had already gone back into the Main Building for a very hot breakfast and free hot chocolate.

As Jenson went over to them as they all sat on the soft brown fabric sofas and they were thankfully laughing, smiling and looking like they had a great night together. He realised he really, really didn't want to talk to them, he didn't want to explain what had happened and his own stupid fears had gotten the better of him.

He noticed Nathan was near the end of a book but it was different to the last one he had noticed at dinner. It was a memoir by a trans man that Nathan seemed completely fascinated by and he was smiling, nodding and even laughing at times quietly to himself.

Like he understood exactly what was going on.

Jenson knew he would never totally get it but it was good that Nathan was okay. Sometimes Jenson just wanted to hug him, protect him and support him no matter what. Yet this time Jenson knew, seriously knew he was only focusing on Nathan so he didn't have to focus on his own problems.

His fears weren't stupid. They were real, valid and it was honestly better for Carter to move up to Scotland single so he could make new friends, get a boyfriend up there and just enjoy life to the fullest without the risk of being dragged down by him.

It was logical, rational and perfect.

"Where's my brother?" Katie asked as he was spotted.

Jenson smiled as he went over to the table and he leant on the back of Nathan's chair. Something that earned him a very annoyed huff.

"Well, it didn't work out," Jenson said.

"Seriously? Yet again," James said. "Yes we know Jacob cheated on you and abandoned you. Yes we understand that Ben had sex with Nathan whilst you were dating and abandoned you. And believe me, we really know Liam was going to pick you up so you could go on holiday together. He never showed and you have no idea what happened to him,"

Jenson nodded. He didn't need to be reminded and judging by the rather annoyed huffing from Nathan he seriously didn't want to be reminded either.

"But you cannot keep breaking up with men out of fear," James said.

Jenson was rather surprised how mature, sensible and manly his big brother was being. He had never seen this side of him at all.

Katie's phone buzzed and it was the dagger-like look that told Jenson that Carter was calling her.

Jenson took her seat. "This is the first time I've ever broken up with a guy. Give me some credit,"

"Really?" Nathan asked clearly too annoyed to continue reading. "That might be true but surely you can admit you have sabotaged all your relationships since Jacob,"

Jenson didn't want to listen to this.

"The only reason that cheating bastard Liam slept with me when I wasn't… my real self was because he wanted someone to care about him. You have always been distant and colder in relationships,"

"Until you met my brother," Katie said.

Jenson got up and moved away from Katie like a scared child as she said bye to James, they kissed and they both promised each other Katie would call as soon as she was home safe.

Katie just shook her head at Jenson. "He loved you,"

Jenson didn't react as Katie walked away and when he looked at James he was surprised to see how concerned he was about her concern.

"I hope you get home safely," James said.

Jenson looked at his parents and no one else was

surprised about the sheer emotion and worry and concern in his voice. James actually cared about her.

"You're a real couple, aren't you?" Jenson asked sitting back down.

James nodded. "Of course, we didn't spend an entire night together for the fun of it. We spoke, had sex and enjoyed our time together. We already have plans to meet up the week after Christmas,"

Jenson laughed and he hugged his brother. He was so proud of James. Before this holiday he had been a player, a bad boyfriend and he never would have been this nice to a girl he had met on holiday, but Katie had clearly caught his interest. And his heart.

The problem was Jenson couldn't deny Carter hadn't done the same to him. Then Jenson had been stupid enough to rip it all up because he was scared about getting cheated on.

"I need to talk to him," Jenson said.

"You better hurry I overheard what Katie was saying on the phone. The Coach is picking them up earlier because they're all packed,"

Jenson just frowned as he saw tens upon tens of people in massive thick coats start to fill into the reception room.

He had no idea how he was going to find beautiful Carter but he seriously had to try. He couldn't let Carter leave without them sorting things out.

It just wasn't right.

CHAPTER 15
17th December 2023
The French Alps, France

Carter really enjoyed the warm feeling of the on-coach heating gently blowing on his face and feet as he sat at the very back of the coach waiting to be taken to the airport, so he could go home without the man he loved. The seats were surprisingly comfortable with its black and red fabric that supported his back perfectly.

Carter sat next to Katie who looked amazing. She looked so happy, positive and like she was having the time of her life. He couldn't have been happier for her and it was great she had found love.

That was actually the hardest part about it all. He would have to see Jenson for the rest of his life, they would have to see each other at James' and Katie's wedding, the birth of their first child and everything after that. It was a nightmare and it was even worse that Carter didn't have a clue about how to fix it all.

"Me and James are going to London together for New Year's," Katie said sounding really excited.

Carter just nodded. He didn't know if his voice could hold itself together if he dared open it.

Instead he simply smiled as a group of young kids and their parents sat in the row in front of them. and the little children started talking about their favourite Christmas music and whether they would see Santa on the way home.

Carter smiled but this was going to be the worst Christmas of his life when he got home. He had had a boyfriend that had dumped him. He was going to be surrounded by Katie phoning James and then his parents kissing and telling each other how much they loved each other.

All whilst he was alone.

Carter didn't even have Jenson's phone number. He was going to grab it earlier at breakfast but then everything had gone to hell.

"You know he's been cheated on before," Katie said as she told him everything James had said.

"Okay," Carter said failing to keep the annoyance out of his voice. He supposed Jenson had the right to feel like that, but surely Jenson knew that he would never ever cheat on him.

Carter loved him. He wanted to live with Jenson, be with him and work in the same city as him.

And that got Carter thinking about the future. What was more important to him? He was still going to get a Masters degree if he stayed in Surrey, he was still going to be able to have the job of his dreams whether he studied in Edinburgh or not.

But he would never ever have another chance with Jenson again. Jenson was a unique person, a wonderful, sexy and amazing man that Carter really, really loved because he could tell they were meant to be together.

And he could even go to live in Edinburgh later on in life, this wasn't a do-or-die moment. But his relationship with Jenson was.

There would be a second chance to live and work in the city of his dreams but there wasn't a second chance to be with Jenson.

He had to talk to Jenson now and if he was stuck here then so be it.

Carter leant over his sister and looked at his mother, who he was now realising had been very normal for a good few hours.

"Why you being so normal?" Carter asked.

"Because," his Mum said, "I don't have a crowd to perform for and I needed you to realise how much you love Jenson,"

Carter shook his head. It was so annoying that his entire family was so much better at relationships than he was and it was even better that he now realised that relationships were all about give and take.

He had to compromise with Jenson so they could stay together, and Carter really needed Jenson to know he would never cheat on him.

Carter got up and went to get off the coach when

it started driving off.

Katie grabbed him to sit him back down and Carter just felt dead inside.

They were driving away from the holiday, from Jenson and most importantly the conversation they so desperately needed to have.

A conversation that might never ever happen now. And their relationship was over without it.

CHAPTER 16
17th December 2023
The French Alps, France

Jenson just felt utterly deflated as he stared at the red coach as it drove away like a bat out of hell. All he wanted was to get on it, talk to beautiful Carter and explain how stupid he had been.

But he was gone.

Jenson didn't know how to contact him, he doubted Katie would let him talk to Carter even if he used James's phone to call her and he didn't even know where in Surrey they lived.

There was no hope.

Jenson just allowed the icy coldness of the French Alps to claim him as his world froze around him. For the first time since he had arrived at the hotel he realised how icy cold the Alps were. Sure there was a strong bite to the air before but now that Carter was gone it was even colder.

Carter really was his sunshine, his light and his

warmth no matter how hot or cold the day. Jenson felt stupid but he had just never ever had these sort of intense, loving feelings towards someone before and he had been stupid enough to throw it all away.

Because he had been scared of something someone else had done to him years ago.

"You can still fix this," Nathan said standing next to Jenson.

Jenson shook his head. He was surprised Nathan wanted to brave the cold like this as a strong wind made the air howl around them. It was only the two of them in the coach park and everyone else was safely inside in the warmth.

"You can still fix this I promise," Nathan said knowing his brother was surprised at him being out in the cold. "You can do whatever you set your mind to, because you're a good person,"

"No I can't fix this. I've ruined it and now I can't even contact him. I can't possibly ask James to call Katie because I would just be ruining his relationship,"

"Do you love him?"

Jenson nodded and he couldn't believe this was actually a question.

"Then you will do whatever it takes,"

Jenson rolled his eyes. It was so annoying that his little brother was wiser, smarter and better at relationships than he was. He had no idea how Nathan was single when he kept saying such clever stuff like that.

"Why do you care?" Jenson asked knowing he had never truly spoken to Nathan about boyfriends before. Sure they had said and debated who were the hottest guys in public and in films and stuff but never boyfriends.

"I care because I love you," Nathan said. "You've supported me, loved me through all of it and you are the only person in this family that has never doubted that I am a man,"

Jenson nodded. He still didn't get what there was to understand about his brother, he didn't have a sister. His brother was his brother and that was that.

"So I want you to be happy and quite frankly I don't want to spend the next week looking after a sulking Jenson. I have a lot of reading to get through and you sulking will only distract me,"

Jenson gently nudged his brother and elbowed him in the ribs. And he went inside to find James.

A few moments later he found his entire family drinking hot chocolates, coffee and some kind of mulled wine mixture with Christmas songs years playing in the background, they were all sitting in silence and resting their feet up on the coffee table in front of the brown fabric sofas.

They looked at Jenson but they didn't say anything and he certainly didn't blame them. Jenson really hoped they were going to back him up here because he needed James more than ever. And with Katie no longer here he really hoped James didn't go back to being his old self.

The idiot brother.

Jenson went over to James and knelt on the ground slightly so they were eye level.

"James," Jenson said really not knowing what to say, "I know we have had our problems over the years. I know when I was straight years and years ago I kissed your girlfriend on purpose. But that's how I knew I was gay,"

James grinned and Jenson realised he really hadn't meant to sound like he was begging.

"I know I have called you a lot of horrible things in the past and we have fought a lot. But if there is anything I can do for you please let me know because I really want you to call Katie please and let me talk with Carter,"

James smiled. "What's your limit?"

"I don't have one," Jenson said before he knew what he was saying. "I'll pay you, clean your house for you, I'll do all your Christmas wrapping for you. Just please let me talk with Carter,"

"Tell me, do you love him?"

Jenson really didn't know what everyone's obsession with that question was.

"Of course I do. Now *please* call Katie," Jenson said.

"Babe," Carter said.

Jenson looked around but he couldn't see Carter, Katie or anyone else from that amazing family. Then James took out his phone and it was on video chat, Jenson took it and smiled and grinned at the beautiful man he really did love.

Jenson knew James had been on video chat the entire time and Carter had heard every single word of it.

"I love you Carter and whatever happens we will get through it," Jenson said feeling more relieved than he had in his entire life.

"I know we will babe because I love you," Carter said feeling just as relieved. "And you're worth changing or adapting my dreams for,"

Jenson had no idea what that meant but as he grabbed a seat next to Nathan, he really looked forward to talking, listening and enjoying Carter's beautiful face even more. And he just knew that they would work things out because they had been snowed in together and their love had developed at first sight.

There certainly wasn't a better way to fall in love than being snowed in together, and Jenson didn't know what was better than a snowy holiday, spending time with family and meeting the love of his life together along the way.

Was there actually a better way to spend a December holiday? Jenson really, really didn't think so.

CHAPTER 17
13th December 2024
The French Alps, France

Carter flat out loved standing on top of a massive ski slope with his sexy, beautiful husband standing next to him in full black, red and orange ski gear. He couldn't believe how perfectly seductive Jenson looked standing next to him as they both prepared to ski down one of the resort's largest and easiest slopes together.

Carter really loved that this slope didn't have any trees, sharp rocks or turns on it, so there shouldn't have been any problems. He hadn't been skiing since last year but Carter really didn't care. He was with the man he loved and that was all that mattered.

As far as he was concerned, the two of them would fall, trip and roll down the slope a little but Carter just knew from the past year that they would be laughing, giggling and enjoying themselves like two teenage lovers.

Life was just perfect whenever he was around Jenson.

Carter really wished the two of them had done some skiing together last year but between the snowstorm, the drama and them explaining why they were going to enjoy doing a long-distance relationship, there simply hadn't been time. And he wasn't exactly sure his legs could take another hard day of skiing after what he had done with Katie the day before his life changed forever.

It was great James and Katie were engaged too and suspecting their first kid together next year. Carter didn't doubt for a second they were going to make amazing parents, and he was seriously glad Nathan had found himself a boyfriend too. And the two of them were seriously cute together.

Carter enjoyed the icy coldness of the gently howling wind around them and grinned at his fiancée (a word he was still loving and getting used to) and scented the scents of damp, pine and mulled wine that lingered in the air.

He would never regret what he had compromised on last Christmas. Carter might not have ended up going to Edinburgh to study, but he still ended up with a good Masters degree, Jenson had moved in and gotten a job in Surrey and they had loved every minute of every day together.

And they were moving to Edinburgh anyway next year, so he could still live, see and work in the city of his dreams.

And in a way, Carter supposed all his fantasies had come true. He still needed to buy a small chandelier for their house but he had found Jenson, his knight, his oxygen and his everything and they had rescued each other in a way. Jenson had rescued Carter from a life without true love, and Carter had saved Jenson from living a life in fear of lovers abandoning him.

They were perfect.

Carter kissed his fiancée one last time and then he pushed himself off the ski slope with Jenson hot on his tail.

And the two lovers laughed, giggled and loved it as they raced each other down the slope. Hoping beyond hope they wouldn't get snowed in again but if they did Carter didn't doubt they would know exactly how to pass the time by doing very creative, adult and intense things to each other.

All night long and the French nights in winter were wonderfully long indeed.

GET YOUR FREE SHORT STORY NOW!
And get signed up to Connor Whiteley's newsletter to hear about new gripping books, offers and exciting projects. (You'll never be sent spam)

https://www.subscribepage.io/gayromancesignup

About the author:

Connor Whiteley is the author of over 60 books in the sci-fi fantasy, nonfiction psychology and books for writer's genre and he is a Human Branding Speaker and Consultant.

He is a passionate warhammer 40,000 reader, psychology student and author.

Who narrates his own audiobooks and he hosts The Psychology World Podcast.

All whilst studying Psychology at the University of Kent, England.

Also, he was a former Explorer Scout where he gave a speech to the Maltese President in August 2018 and he attended Prince Charles' 70th Birthday Party at Buckingham Palace in May 2018.

Plus, he is a self-confessed coffee lover!

Other books by Connor Whiteley:

Bettie English Private Eye Series

A Very Private Woman

The Russian Case

A Very Urgent Matter

A Case Most Personal

Trains, Scots and Private Eyes

The Federation Protects

Cops, Robbers and Private Eyes

Just Ask Bettie English

An Inheritance To Die For

The Death of Graham Adams

Bearing Witness

The Twelve

The Wrong Body

The Assassination Of Bettie English

Wining And Dying

Eight Hours

Uniformed Cabal

A Case Most Christmas

Gay Romance Novellas

Breaking, Nursing, Repairing A Broken Heart

Jacob And Daniel

Fallen For A Lie

Spying And Weddings

Clean Break

Awakening Love
Meeting A Country Man
Loving Prime Minister
Snowed In Love
Never Been Kissed
Love Betrays You
Love And Hurt

Lord of War Origin Trilogy:
Not Scared Of The Dark
Madness
Burn Them All

Way Of The Odyssey
Odyssey of Rebirth
Convergence of Odysseys
Odyssey Of Hope

Lady Tano Fantasy Adventure Stories
Betrayal
Murder
Annihilation

The Fireheart Fantasy Series
Heart of Fire
Heart of Lies
Heart of Prophecy

Heart of Bones
Heart of Fate

City of Assassins (Urban Fantasy)
City of Death
City of Martyrs
City of Pleasure
City of Power

Agents of The Emperor
Return of The Ancient Ones
Vigilance
Angels of Fire
Kingmaker
The Eight
The Lost Generation
Hunt
Emperor's Council
Speaker of Treachery
Birth Of The Empire
Terraforma
Spaceguard

The Rising Augusta Fantasy Adventure Series
Rise To Power
Rising Walls
Rising Force

Rising Realm

Lord Of War Trilogy (Agents of The Emperor)
Not Scared Of The Dark
Madness
Burn It All Down

Miscellaneous:
Dead Names
RETURN
FREEDOM
SALVATION
Reflection of Mount Flame
The Masked One
The Great Deer
English Independence

OTHER SHORT STORIES BY CONNOR WHITELEY

Mystery Short Story Collections
Criminally Good Stories Volume 1: 20 Detective Mystery Short Stories
Criminally Good Stories Volume 2: 20 Private Investigator Short Stories
Criminally Good Stories Volume 3: 20 Crime Fiction Short Stories

Criminally Good Stories Volume 4: 20 Science Fiction and Fantasy Mystery Short Stories
Criminally Good Stories Volume 5: 20 Romantic Suspense Short Stories

Connor Whiteley Starter Collections:
Agents of The Emperor Starter Collection
Bettie English Starter Collection
Matilda Plum Starter Collection
Gay Romance Starter Collection
Way Of The Odyssey Starter Collection
Kendra Detective Fiction Starter Collection

Mystery Short Stories:
Protecting The Woman She Hated
Finding A Royal Friend
Our Woman In Paris
Corrupt Driving
A Prime Assassination
Jubilee Thief
Jubilee, Terror, Celebrations
Negative Jubilation
Ghostly Jubilation
Killing For Womenkind
A Snowy Death
Miracle Of Death

A Spy In Rome
The 12:30 To St Pancreas
A Country In Trouble
A Smokey Way To Go
A Spicy Way To GO
A Marketing Way To Go
A Missing Way To Go
A Showering Way To Go
Poison In The Candy Cane
Kendra Detective Mystery Collection Volume 1
Kendra Detective Mystery Collection Volume 2
Mystery Short Story Collection Volume 1
Mystery Short Story Collection Volume 2
Criminal Performance
Candy Detectives
Key To Birth In The Past

Science Fiction Short Stories:
Their Brave New World
Gummy Bear Detective
The Candy Detective
What Candies Fear
The Blurred Image
Shattered Legions
The First Rememberer

Life of A Rememberer
System of Wonder
Lifesaver
Remarkable Way She Died
The Interrogation of Annabella Stormic
Blade of The Emperor
Arbiter's Truth
Computation of Battle
Old One's Wrath
Puppets and Masters
Ship of Plague
Interrogation
Edge of Failure

<u>Fantasy Short Stories:</u>
City of Snow
City of Light
City of Vengeance
Dragons, Goats and Kingdom
Smog The Pathetic Dragon
Don't Go In The Shed
The Tomato Saver
The Remarkable Way She Died
Dragon Coins
Dragon Tea
Dragon Rider

All books in 'An Introductory Series':
Clinical Psychology and Transgender Clients
Clinical Psychology
Moral Psychology
Myths About Clinical Psychology
401 Statistics Questions For Psychology Students
Careers In Psychology
Psychology of Suicide
Dementia Psychology
Clinical Psychology Reflections Volume 4
Forensic Psychology of Terrorism And Hostage-Taking
Forensic Psychology of False Allegations
Year In Psychology
CBT For Anxiety
CBT For Depression
Applied Psychology
BIOLOGICAL PSYCHOLOGY 3RD EDITION
COGNITIVE PSYCHOLOGY THIRD EDITION
SOCIAL PSYCHOLOGY- 3RD EDITION
ABNORMAL PSYCHOLOGY 3RD EDITION
PSYCHOLOGY OF RELATIONSHIPS- 3RD EDITION

DEVELOPMENTAL PSYCHOLOGY 3ᴿᴰ EDITION
HEALTH PSYCHOLOGY
RESEARCH IN PSYCHOLOGY
A GUIDE TO MENTAL HEALTH AND TREATMENT AROUND THE WORLD- A GLOBAL LOOK AT DEPRESSION
FORENSIC PSYCHOLOGY
THE FORENSIC PSYCHOLOGY OF THEFT, BURGLARY AND OTHER CRIMES AGAINST PROPERTY
CRIMINAL PROFILING: A FORENSIC PSYCHOLOGY GUIDE TO FBI PROFILING AND GEOGRAPHICAL AND STATISTICAL PROFILING.
CLINICAL PSYCHOLOGY
FORMULATION IN PSYCHOTHERAPY
PERSONALITY PSYCHOLOGY AND INDIVIDUAL DIFFERENCES
CLINICAL PSYCHOLOGY REFLECTIONS VOLUME 1
CLINICAL PSYCHOLOGY REFLECTIONS VOLUME 2
Clinical Psychology Reflections Volume 3
CULT PSYCHOLOGY
Police Psychology

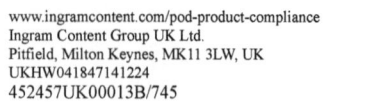